Sunday Edition

By

JW Kelley

This little ditty is for you, Wild Bill, better known as William Pepy, 1st Grade Detective, NYCPD, the real deal with 32 years on the force. It was a true honor.

This book is a work of fiction. Names, characters, places, and incidents are either products of the author's imagination or are used fictitiously. Any resemblance to actual events, locales or persons, living or deceased, is entirely coincidental.

© 2021

Manufactured in the USA

Create Space Independent Publishing Platform

North Charleston, SC

ISBN: 9798406669860

LCCN: 2022903041

Novels by JW Kelley

The Strange Adventures of Brent and Bonnie Blue

When the Devil Comes Calling… (The Trilogy)

24th Precinct/The Heartsick Killer

Night Riders of Sheridan

Five Vets and a Funeral

Yesterday's Tomorrow

The Astronaut's Twin

Shadows in the Dark

Corporal Gallagher

Smile of Affection

Dreamer's Market

Dog-Eared Books

Manny and Ralph

Starbucks Corner

Cyclotron Factor

Words & Phrases

Long Way Back

Sunday Edition

Fortune Teller

Pages in Time

Novels by JW Kelley

Two Buckets

Mind Reader

Curious Tale

Laundromat

Time Slider

Will Power

$38 Billion

Killer Five

Time Loop

The Novel

Mukaluks

Desert 91

The Attic

Alley Cat

Stranger

Code 99

Howard

Conjure

Castles

Publications may be purchased online

Barnes&Noble.com

KindleBooks.com

Amazon.com

MEETING

Joyce Miller lived with her parents on Delmonico Street, a couple of blocks from Andrew Peck and his folk's home on North West Cambridge Street. She had been there most of her life, but following college and because of Mr. and Mrs. Miller's advancing age, she decided to move back to the city and live in an apartment close to her parents.

Joyce and Andrew knew each other from the old neighborhood and high school but ran with different crowds. She was a pleasant-looking young girl who became more attractive as she matured into adulthood. However, Andrew was always a little gangly and somewhat of an odd duck, but she couldn't figure how or why? Her friends called him weird, and maybe he was.

On a Saturday afternoon, while they were both grocery shopping, they accidentally bumped into each other in the soup section at the local Trader Joe's Store.

"Hey, Joyce, how are you? And how are your folks?" 'Will she remember me from high school or the neighborhood?' he wondered as he stood looking at the nice-looking woman. He took a deep breath to calm himself. But it wasn't working, for his heart was thumping like a jackhammer.

"Hi Andrew, how are you? I'm doing good and I finally have a job. As for my parents, they are getting older, as I'm sure yours are too."

"Well," he stammered. "My folks had an automobile accident a year after we graduated from high school and died at the scene. You probably didn't hear about it, for you were in college by then."

"Oh, God! That's awful; I'm so sorry," she flushed scarlet with embarrassment for not knowing about his parent's death.

"That's okay," he started as he looked off into the distance for a few seconds. "It was a long time ago now, a long time ago," he continued slowly, eyes tearing.

Andrew looked at Joyce and said, "the mind is an amazing thing, especially the way it can shut out grief and find a way to cope and go on with life. On a more pleasant note, it's so nice to see you again. Maybe we will see each other again sometime. I believe you live in the Belvedere apartments?"

"Yes, I do," 'how does he know?' She pondered.

She felt his stomach tighten when he asked, "May I stop by sometime to talk about old times?" he could hear her breathe and felt a tingle on the back of his neck with anticipation.

Joyce hesitated for a brief moment but relented and said, "Sure, that would be nice."

They both went their different way. Joyce went through the closest checked-out counter and headed back to her apartment. 'He still seems a bit weird, but I can never put my finger on the weirdness... maybe it's me?'

Several days later, there was a knock at Joyce's apartment door. She opened it, and there stood Andrew Peck grinning with a bottle of red wine in his hands.

"Is this a good time?" he asked, swaying back and forth on his feet. Andrew stood stiffly, hand in a pocket, waiting but with a glimmer of hope that she would ask him in.

"Ah, sure. Why not? Come on in, Andrew. It's nice to see you again."

'There's just something queer about this man now and back when we were teenagers.'

Joyce opened the bottle of wine.

"To our parent," he said, clinking her glass with his. "Be they alive or dead."

'Odd toast,' she thought.

But stated, "to our parents."

ZERO

The wine is good," said Joyce, sitting back down on the couch but on the opposite end. After about an hour of small talk and when the bottle of wine finished, Joyce got up and motioned toward the door.

Instead of getting up, Andrew grabbed the woman flung her back down. He immediately pulled her legs toward the other end of the couch and sprang onto her like a cat.

"What are you doing, Andrew? Stop, stop!" she screamed as she clawed at the man now sitting astride of her.

"I'm sorry, Joyce, but I need to know how it feels. I'm sorry!"

"What?" she yelled at the top of her lungs while hitting at him with all of her might. None of this did any good, for the man weighed too much and was very strong. However, Joyce did manage to scratch Andrew's face and arms getting tiny pieces of tissue underneath her fingernails in the process.

Andrew casually picked up the pillow above her head and immediately placed it over her face. All the while, she was squirming and fighting franticly for her life. He leaned on the pillow with all of his weight and could feel her strength weakening as he continued to apply pressure.

'How long does it take?' he wondered, still on top of her while pushing down as hard as he could, thus blocking her mouth and nose from any air.

After several minutes she was quiet and no longer moved. Andrew still held the pad on her face... just in case.

Slowly he removed the cushion and looked at her. She was no longer breathing, and the strangest thing, he looked down at his crotch, and he had a boner that was as hard as a rock. He unzipped his trousers and lifted out his throbbing penis. He calmly put on a condom and pulled her pants down. She was still warm as he pumped several times ejaculating into the rubber.

"Not too bad, Joyce... but you need to move a little more and not lie there like a log." He laughed at his joke.

Andrew wiped himself off threw the rubber in a small plastic bag he brought.   He then took out a lint roller from his pocket and rolled it all over the divan and floor near him.

"It looks clean to me," he said to the empty room.

The apartment was silent, but a quality of silence that unnerved him and made him feel panicky.

He checked the area, picking up the empty wine bottle, the cork, and the two glasses he put into the plastic bag. Next, Andrew took a cloth from the kitchen and polished the table they had used and as well as everything else he might have touched.

Still using the cloth, Andrew turned on the television to a soap opera and quietly left the apartment.

CHAPTER 1

Jenny Holland was a twenty-two-year-old graduate of the University of Oregon, Eugene, with a degree in business. After securing a position in accounting with International Business Machines, IBM's office in New York. Jenny was excited to start a new life in the huge municipality.

Her parents pleaded for her to stay until Monday, but it was no deal. Jenney was anxious to start her new life and immediately left Springfield, Oregon, to make her way to the city that never sleeps.

The first few days in the city, her head was continually turned up, staring at the tall wonderments of the skyscraper buildings. "The only thing taller than these in Oregon," she said out loud, "is Mount Hood in Portland."

After Jenny searched and searched for an apartment, she finally found a tiny flat in Manhattan at 513 West 173rd street. It certainly was not what she was expecting, for the apartment had 750 total square feet of space or roughly the same size as her bedroom in Springfield. The flat was small, but the price was large, far more than she wanted to pay at $1650.00 per month, but what do you do?

"It's the city," she decided.

Nevertheless, she was ecstatic to be out of the house and on her own.

However, it was a lonely place even with the millions of people scurrying to and from wherever they were scurrying. Gladys, a colleague at Jenny's work, suggested she look at the personals in the New York Times newspaper and perhaps hook up with some nice guy or check out the numerous single websites on the internet. "That's how I met Matt," she declared, smiling, "and it's better than hanging out at the bar scene."

She did not want to go to a singles website electing instead to try the newspaper's personals. In the Times, she noticed a simple ad that read... *Alone and lonely, 29yo male.*

Jenny thought about the ad for several days... *Alone and lonely, 29yo male.* She responded to the advertisement with, *also alone and lonely, 22yo female,* but added her West 173rd Street address and waited.

A few days later, she received a lovely note from a Gary Sawyer. Every other day after that, she received another and another letter. She enjoyed reading the short correspondences but was curious why he did not call. His odd instruction was specific, suggesting she keep the messages together, which numbered five so far.

However, like clockwork, she sat near her apartment window waiting for the mailman. And today, there he was. She lingered until hearing the postman place the mail in the various boxes near the complex's front door. She opened her door and raced down the one flight of stairs to her mailbox as soon as he was gone.

The thick man stood in the shadows at the other end of the corridor, waiting patiently as the young girl hurried out of her apartment. She left the door open and scampered to get her mail. He quickly walked down the hall to the flat and into a closet where he remained. The man carried a small rope he fiddled with as he waited. He smiled as the unsuspecting woman returned with his letter in her hand.

CHAPTER 2

The 36-year-old New York City police Detective, 2nd Grade Felix Muhammad Sullivan was on his hands and knees searching through the final crime scene's evidence bags. The detective had 12 plastic containers spread out all over his small office floor as he rummaged through each one of them again. He had seen something early in his search that sparked his curiosity, but now he could not remember what or why. Thus, he was scrounging into every container once again to find whatever it was he had seen, but lost it as if a leaf in an autumn breeze.

"I'm either losing my fuckin' mind, or it's early-stage dementia?" He stared at the sacks and wondered what had tweaked his interest, momentarily catching him off guard mentally.

The rag and bones man moaned as he moved about,

continuing to search every bag once again. He resembled a homeless person scavenging as fast as possible, for that last scrap of special worth.

Suddenly, he looked up more frazzled than before and immediately stopped. Felix wrapped his arms tightly around his knees that jutted up sharply and shook his head as if to see if it would rattle... it didn't. His face was pale and unshaven, making him look worn out and older than his age. His raven dark hair was uncombed, his shirt had coffee stains on the front and unbuttoned at the neck. His knees were dirty and nearly worn through, the once shinny shoes were scuffed on the toes from crawling from container to container.

"What the fuck's going on in here, Irish?" bellowed a loud, blustery voice of the precinct's Lieutenant Washington, a big black man who had been a policeman for nearly 30 years and counting. "And when was the last time you left this rat hole?" he quizzed, surveying the room. "And this place smells like shit. When did you last take a shower?" he continued, plugging his nose and shaking his head in disgust.

"Hey, LT. Sorry. Well, I've been here for five days and nights, as for the shower? I guess last week sometime." He smelled his stained underarms. "Yep, I do smell ripe," he answered. "If you have a minute, I'd like to run something by you?" He looked up to his superior and waited.

About that time, another detective stuck his head in the door and asked, "Are we havin' the meeting in here this morning, LT? God Damn, Irish, this place smells like a pigsty. By the way, a couple of the new guys wanted me to ask you why you're called, Irish? They said your first name is Felix, which is Mexican, and you ain't no spic, your second name is Muhammad, and you certainly ain't no Arab, and your last name is Sullivan, and you certainly ain't no potato eater..."

"Fuck you and the new guys, Dombrowski!" returned Irish, smiling. "Tell'em I'm a God Damn New York City police Detective 2nd Grade!" He chuckled and waved his hand.

"Okay, I'll relay the message." he laughed and left.

"Okay, Irish, whaddya got?"

CHAPTER 3

Felix was still on his knees as he rearranged the 11 crime scene evidence bags and one empty plastic container. He first made eleven slips of paper with the numbers one through eleven written on each and a big zero for the empty one. Next, he placed the one slip on the first evidence cases bag until he ended with the 11th. Next, he moved the last bag he named zero, out in front.

"In the first crime scene evidence bag from the young lady we call number one had a *Sunday Edition* of the New York Times in her apartment."

"So?" he burst out, questioning the detective harshly.

"*Sunday Edition* is the only day of the week the New York Times prints personal advertising, such as single sites... ah, ya know lookin' for love in all the wrong places as Johnny Lee's song goes. Or maybe looking for love on the internet. I discovered a slight fingernail indentation beside a personal ad reading, *Alone and lonely, 29yo male.* Several of the other eleven, not counting our zero, took the Times, but there were no newspapers found where they were murdered, which I also find interesting."

The precinct's lieutenant was now down on the floor beside the detective, watching his every move.

"He places a personal ad in *Sunday Edition* of the Times, and they respond with their address. He probably corresponds with them and the next thing you know they either allow him in or he sneaks in and they are dead by strangulation with a rope and in their own apartment," stated Felix, smiling, leaning back on splayed hands.

"That's how he finds them... personal ads in the Sunday Edition of the New York God Damn Times?" stated the lieutenant now on his feet, face flushing crimson.

"Yep! And, 22-year-old Jenny Holland from somewhere in bumfuck Oregon was his 11th or should I say his 12th?"

He stared ahead, his throat tightening; no air in his lungs, a cold hard claw curling through his chest as adrenaline surged through his body from intense anger. "Yep!" he repeated.

The senior officer got up from the floor, brushed off his trousers and said, "Good job, Irish, but what do you mean by his 12th?"

"I don't think number one was his first! It was a chance meeting with zero and he acted impulsively and killed her."

"What?" questioned the lieutenant in a gruff exasperated voice. "Why?"

"Do you remember back about four and a half years ago, a young lady on Delmonico Street was found murdered in her apartment?"

"Yeah, smothered, you wrote in your report if I remember correctly?"

"Right. When we arrived at the scene we found some guy out in front of the building sobbing and pacing in circles, hands on his head, crunching over as if in belly pain?"

"And?"

"It turned out to be the victim's brother. Evidently, they had been very close and the guy was taking her death very hard."

"Yeah, I remember reading that."

"Well, the man was yelling and screaming while several officers tried to comfort him as the crowd continued to grow.

I made my way into the house to see the victim and it appeared she had been smothered. Returning outside, I first pushed back the sidewalk gawkers and went back to talk to the brother. He was obviously still upset as I stood looking at him.

The man squatted down and put his hands up, palms out and said, "give me a few minutes, please, I'll be okay, it's just," and then he put his face in his hands and sobbed more.

"Okay," replied the boss.

"Well, he was sobbing so hard it was difficult to understand him, but he did mention a neighbor, she knew from high school, who lived several blocks away on North West Cambridge Street. I asked why him? Do you think he might have killed her? He looked up at me and immediately stop crying and in a totally different tone said, the guys a weird fuckin' duck. He even has tits like a girl and walks... well, you know?"

"So?" questioned the boss, looking at the detective.

"So, it was nothing. No rap sheet, no links to the victim, other than attending the same high school as the girl along with 500 other students. But looking back at the tit boy, he was different like the brother said," answered Felix, picking up a rubber band and twisting it round his fingers. He cocked his head and squinted, his eyebrows rolling into the shape of a fuzzy v. "Different," he repeated in a whisper.

"Okay?"

"LT. our killer had his initial taste nearly four and a half years ago when, I believe, he smothered his first victim with a pillow. She obviously put up a fight, but it was a trial run for him."

The lieutenant bobbed his head.

"Try to imagine, if you will, attempting to smother someone. Jesus Christ, LT. it would be extremely difficult pushing down on the pillow and the other person is clawing and kicking with all of her might to get loose and not die. At the same time, she's screaming and yelling and you're hoping no one hears you. Maybe she kicks, bites you or claws you, in the process of trying to get free."

"Now what?"

"The man got a taste of what it's like, and evidently, enjoyed the thrill of the kill. This was his first, and he decided not to smother the next, for it was too difficult, and they might escape. So, he changed his MO and started to use a rope he had to carry. This way, he could watch the victim's squirm, their faces flushing red followed by pinpoints red spots under the skin as their eyes and eyelids, become bloodshot. Ultimately their face swells, turns blue, and their eyes bug out from the backup of blood followed by unconsciousness which occurs within seconds and death within minutes."

"And?"

"I believe zero was his first, not number one. Zero was the closest to his regular stomping grounds or where he lived. After zero, this hunter move to a different quarry for his next lamb. Much further away from zero and into the city."

CHAPTER 4

Felix could still remember seeing the *Sunday Edition's* zero kill and what she looked like after he had smothered her.

Asphyxiation by smothering is caused by blocking the air entry to the lungs and with the simultaneous closure of the nose and mouth. It's not a pretty sight. It's horrible!

They were bruises on this young lady with abrasions on her cheeks, around her mouth, lips, and several lesions. All of which were typical for such a victim.

"Don't think about the fucker, Irish," said Detective 2nd Grade, Dombrowski, Sullivan's partner for the last five years. "We'll get him sooner or later. Now drink up. I don't want to see you moping around. We're supposed to have fun. It's Friday, for fuck sake, and it's time to howl at the moon!"

Sullivan showed a flicker of a smile, "Yeah, yeah,

but..."

"No buts, Irish unless you're checkin' out the cute red-head on the other end of the bar. She's glanced this way twice. But, maybe she's checking me out?"

"Right!"

The both laughed as they watched another guy make a move on her and she seemed to be enjoying the attention.

"Bastard!"

"Right!"

Harvey, a short, chubby man with a drinker's red nose and ratty gray hair, walked up and sat down beside Dombrowski. "What's up, guys? Friday night?"

The other two bobbed their heads in sequence. "Yep, just chillin'. What going on with Narcotic?" asked Sullivan.

"Snortin' squirtin', and diein' as fast as they can get that Fentanyl shit. It always amazes me how many overdoses we get every day of the year. When they leave their residence, they should take a tab of Narcan to prevent any adverse outcomes that evening."

The other two laughed at the sick joke, which was true.

"What are ya drinkin'"? asked Dombrowski. "Irish is buying."

"Two fingers GlenDronach 12," barked Thompson to the bartender, showing his two fingers stretching out proudly. "Thanks, Irish."

"My pleasure, Clyde."

"Anything new on the *Sunday Edition* guy? Narcotics heard you might have something concrete?" The man rubbed his crimson nose, took a sip, and smacked his lips to the taste of the fine Scotch.

"You know homicide, we always have a clue even when we don't."

An elderly woman sat down at the other end of the Bars and Stars Tavern and gave the trio a big gap tooth smile.

"Is that what it's gonna be like to get old?" asked Dombrowski shaking his head.

"You mean, smiling at three handsome detectives?"

"Fuck you, Clyde."

"Just saying." They all giggled.

The old lady asked the bartender for an old-fashion and started chewing on a strip of stale beef jerky.

Several hours later, Felix got up stretched his arms, and said, "I'm headin' home."

"Yeah, me too, echoed Hank Dombrowski. What about you Clyde?"

"Nah, I'm gonna stay a while longer. See ya."

The two detectives, both a little tight, left their favorite bar. "Fun, Irish, thanks!"

"You bet, partner. Tomorrow?"

"Tomorrow."

Back at his one-bedroom apartment, Felix dropped onto the well-used couch and studied the wall covered with clippings and various other information on the *Sunday Edition* killer.

He felt a soft flutter in his stomach. "How does he decide who and where to kill these you ladies? Does he find them at bars, restaurants, sex clubs? No to all the above. They are young, mostly new to the city, and probably lonely. But he does lure them to him one way or another."

"Bastard!" he growled to himself. "What are you doing tonight? Planning your next kill, or maybe you're like everyone else... out chasing whatever it is you chase. Your preference might be... I bet you're a fuckin' homo or have a latent mental problem about your mother. What is it?" His words hung in the air like an Oregon fog.

"I will find you! Sooner or later!"

CHAPTER 5

Andrew Peck, age 34, pulled the curtain back and peeked out the window of his home at 6755 North West Cambridge Street. He moved the fake walker he used anytime he left the house, no matter when. He portrayed an elderly man by wearing an authentic looking wig and hat, bent black plastic frame glasses and extra-large nondescript clothing purchased at a nearby thrift store. He also wore oversized shoes with a rock in the left providing him with a realistic limp. 'I don't want to forget my limp while walking, so they do hurt my feet producing a genuine laming shuffle.'

"Now, I look like all the other welfare senior citizens making their way around the city," he said to himself while smiling.

However, in his right-hand jacket pocket was a Sig P365 9mm handgun and a rope, "just in case," he whispered, "for there's a lot of bad people out there who'll try to take advantage of the elderly."

He only had to walk a block to the corner mom and pop store. They appreciated his patronage over the last few years.

He nodded to the elderly Chinese owner as he hobbled into the store and waited hanging tight to the walker as he shook.

"You're open too late, Mr. Chin," stated Andrew in his well-practiced old person's voice. "You should be home with your family," he continued, smiling.

"Oh, yes, I know. But to put food on the table I must be open seven days a week from six a.m. to 9 p.m. to survive. Rent is high for this little store and the owner continues to raise it every year."

"I hear you," he faked a throaty cough followed by a loud snort.

Two men suddenly rushed into the small shop and raced to the counter. "Give us all your money, old man!" yelled one of them as he swished a big knife toward the clerk. He leaned over closer to the Chinese owner and screamed, "hurry up, or I'll cut ya! You fuckin' slope!"

Mr. Chin was shaking like a leaf as he fumbled to open the cash-register. "I'm hurrying, kind sir," he was able to say.

The other man glanced back at Andrew and smirked noticing the old man holding tight to his walker with the apparatus shaking as if the elderly gentleman had severe tremors.

Andrew was standing statue still as he slowly reached into his pocket and touched the Sig P365 9mm handgun.

He pushed the walker to the side, stepped back and pulled out the 9mm weapon. "Back away from the counter, Gentlemen, and put your hands behind your head, otherwise, I'll shoot you both where you stand! And I mean now!" he ordered in an overly loud voice of authority.

Both men whirled around and stared at what they thought was another feeble senior citizen. However, he was no longer old, for Andrew had removed his hat, wig, and bent glasses and was holding the weapon in a modified two-handed stance preparing to fire if needed.

"What's it going to be, assholes, dead or alive? It

makes no difference to me."

"Mr. Chin, call 911 and tell the station an officer needs assistance and give him your address. Do it now, Mr. Chin!" he ordered sounding official.

The old clerk, mouth open in wonderment, but quickly dialed the number and watched.

"On your knees, hands behind your head, fingers interlocked. You know the drill! You have the right to remain silent. Anything you say can and will be used against you in a court of law. You have the right to an attorney. If you cannot afford an attorney, one will be provided for you. Do you understand the rights I have just told you?"

Both men bobbed their heads as blaring sirens could be heard in the background.

Moments later, two uniform officers' race into Mr. Chin's store just as Andrew exited the back.

"Where's the police officer?" asked one.

The owner of the store shrugged his shoulders and shook his head in wonderment?

"Check the back of the store," ordered one policeman, to the other. "Make sure the guys not wounded or something."

"Got it!"

The other officer touched his mobile phone and said, "Central, there is no police officer here in need of assistance, however, we did interrupt a robbery in progress."

Static, "Sir, an officer requested assistance at your current location and you responded to that call... correct?"

"Yes, Ma'am and we are here providing assistance as you requested and arrested two robbery suspects." He smirked and shook his head.

CHAPTER 6

A woman, dressed to the nines, entered the NYPD headquarters at 1 Police Plaza, located on Park Row in Lower Manhattan near City Hall. She was sobbing uncontrollably while rubbing her heavily made-up face smudging her red rouge cheeks and black mascara eyes.

"He tried to kill me!" she sniveled, while covering her face and complaining to the front desk sergeant. "My boyfriend placed a rope around my neck while making love to me, and he would have murdered me if I hadn't punched him in the gut!" she screamed.

The sergeant made a quick call to the homicide division and asked for Detective Sullivan. "Detective, Macmillan here, I have a woman here who claims her boyfriend tried to choke her with a rope. Kinda sounds like that *Sunday Edition* guy you notified everyone about. Just thought you'd like to know."

"Thanks, Mac," replied Felix.

The elderly police officer manning the front desk had sparse hair, protruding belly and was nearing retirement. He thought he had seen and heard everything during his long tenure as a police officer, but he was wrong.

The sergeant turned his attention back to the woman and asked, "Was he tryin' to muff ya or snuff ya?" he quizzed with a slight grin.

"The skinny fucker was tryin' to choke me to death with a rope!" she screeched at the top of her lungs, her face flushing scarlet with her black eye makeup smeared and running down her cheeks. "I want you to arrest the fucker!" she continued banging her fist on the desk.

"Calm down, Miss..."

"It's O'Malley, Frank O'Malley. I'm not a total woman, ah, not yet, though in the process of becoming one. I'm considered to be transgendering,' she boasted. "My body is mostly female from the hormones, and of course, I dress accordingly, but I haven't consented to the penile inversion."

"What the fuck is a penile inversion?" questioned the old policeman, who appeared puzzled.

"Ya know, the penis is turned inside out to form the inner walls of the vagina. The head of the penis is then used to create a clitoris. Outer and inner labia are formed, and the urethra is shortened and repositioned."

The police sergeant paled, stood up, put up his hands while shaking his head, "Stop! Stop! Too much information, too much information! I don't want or care to hear about any inside-out pecker!" He shook his head negatively and sat back down, frustrated.

"What I want to know is did this person try to kill ya or was it ruff love? Should I have him arrested and sent straight to Riker?"

The man/woman nonchalantly sashay about the front lobby for a few seconds, placed her hands on her hips, presenting a stereotypical display and flair of a homosexual. She smiled with her wide red lips and bellied up to the officer's desk for a few moments. She puckered her mouth and answered, "Heaven's no. Just scare him a little."

The officer turned and bellowed, "Off with you!

Next!"

Detective Sullivan came out to the front desk and asked, "So, whatcha got, Mac?"

"I thought it might be the Sunday Edition guy, but turned out be two homos doin' their thing. Sorry to have bothered you, Detective."

"No, bother, Mac, thanks."

"Anything?" asked Sullivan's partner, Dombrowski.

"Nah, Macmillan thought he might have heard something, but it was nothing." Felix returned to his computer screen checking to see the *Sunday Edition* and if anymore girls were strangled. There were none.

CHAPTER 7

Hazel Hampton was from a small farming community of Le Claire, Iowa, a charming town outside of Des Moines with a population of 3,765.

Miss Hampton was a pleasant young woman with the same stature as her father, combined with the athletic abilities of her mother. She was 6'1" and 175 pounds, resulting in a very statuesque but sturdy physique. Hazel had four brothers whom she wrestled with all of her life, thus was used to brawling until going to The University of Iowa in Iowa City, Iowa.

She received a full scholarship for track and field arena as a shotput thrower where she excelled. She received national attention from several multi-sporting event organizations. However, following graduation, with a degree Petroleum Engineering, she elected to forgo more track and field endeavors and search for an engineering job.

"Where are you going to look for work?" her advisor asked.

Hazel placed a hand on a hip, tilted her head, and smiled. "I've been thinking about looking in New York City," she returned, fiddling with the small folding pocket knife her dad gave her years ago, which she always carried.

"It's a big city but it can be lonely."

"With all of those millions of people?"

"Yep, even with all of those millions,"

"I've always lived in a small town. The University is larger than Le Claire. So, it's the city." Another grin. "I've gotten several offers, and I believe I'll take the Gulf Institution's offer."

"Be careful. New York is not as safe as Le Claire."

"Thank you."

"Good luck, Hazel."

CHAPTER 8

New York City police Detective 2nd Grade Felix Muhammad Sullivan, sat staring at his blank computer screen as Detective 2nd Grade Dombrowski marched into the man's tiny office. "Whatcha doing, Irish?"

Felix's eyes appeared glazed over as he glanced up to his friend. "Reality is setting in, Dom, and I'm stumped! How in the fuck are we gonna catch this bastard?" He shook his head in frustration.

"Well," he started, shrugging his shoulders, I don't know?"

"The fucker's well organized, watchin' and waitin' for his next victim."

"To do what?"

"To place another fuckin' ad in the personals."

"He'll place the ad and watch."

"But I'm watchin' too!"

"Does the lab have anything at all?"

"A single strand of hair from his first, more than four years ago, but there wasn't any match in the data bank. Strange, she probably clawed him, but her fingernails were as clean as if done by a professional manicurist."

"Pubic hair?"

Felix shook his head negatively. "Nope. Hair from his head or his fuckin' nose." A leer.

"How long has it been since he got that Holland girl?"

"Three fuckin' weeks. And I know he's getting ready and itchin' for another."

"Any theories about the killer?"

"Between 20 and 30. Probably a high school graduate, lives in the city or close, has no family, or should I say, he's not married. Has a menial, but steady job... maybe? He's emotionally disturbed, but not enough for us regular folks to notice? He might have had a problem with his peers or was possible assaulted as a youth."

He frowned. "Typical deviate beginning shit! He'll probably cry for his mommy when I arrest his ass and throw him in the slammer. They always do. Fuckin' pussies."

Dombrowski nodded his head. "Well, good luck, Irish!" He returned to his own cubical.

CHAPTER 9

The NYPD is the largest and one of the oldest police departments in the United States. The headquarters is at 1 Police Plaza, located on Park Row in Lower Manhattan near City Hall. And there sat Detective Sullivan, working on a Sunday in his tiny office, eyes staring at the computer, with an occasional glance outside. 'Today is Sunday, and here I am twiddling my thumbs,' he reflected, noticing his image in the window. He stuck his tongue out at the doppelgänger.

A young newly commissioned patrolman hurried up to the precinct's lieutenant's office and asked a question. The lieutenant signaled toward Felix and the rookie policeman turned and rushed where pointed.

"Sunday Times, Detective," stated the man, and stood waiting as if a child wanting a reward.

Felix glanced up and smiled... remembering when he too had graduated from the police academy and wanted nothing more than to make a good impression. "Ah, thanks," he looked at the man's name tag, "Officer Langston."

The officer grinned with satisfaction, turned, and rushed away.

CHAPTER 10

Police Detective 2nd Grade Felix Muhammad Sullivan immediately opened the newspaper and began to search the personal ads. And there is was, *Alone and lonely, 29yo male* with a number only the advertiser and newspaper could read and respond.

"LT. we need a search warrant to the Times personals," pleaded the detective to his boss. "Four years we've been after the *Sunday Edition* killer, LT. and we desperately need a warrant." Sullivan put his hands together and wrung them as if wet... they were not. "We get our first real break and the Times won't budge."

"Talk to Judge Meyers; maybe he'll give you a break, and again, maybe not. Your call, Detective Sullivan."

After an hour of sitting in his office, Felix got up and said, "Okay, I'll do it!"

"Just be careful of what you say, Irish," said Dombrowski. "He's a tough old buzzard!"

"Yeah, yeah!" He returned, sounding exasperated.

CHAPTER 11

Two hours later, Felix stood in front of the tough old buzzard pleading his case. "But sir..."

The elderly judge sat low in his chair, looking more child-like than an officiating New York City judge. He raised his hand, palm out. There was an immediate hush in the man's massive office as if God had commanded the silence.

"You're certain of what you're saying, Detective Sullivan, that this *Sunday Edition* killer, as you call him, will soon strike the *24yo Iowa farm girl, who is also alone and lonely* as written in Sunday's personals?"

The man bobbed his head and was silent, knowing the judge disliked too much talking.

"And she, whoever she is, knows nothing?"

Another nod of the detective's head.

"What again do you want from the newspaper?"

"Names and addresses. Nothing more." Responded Sullivan, his emotions churning like cats in a gunny sack headed for the water.

And now he waited anxiously for the judge's response.

'One Mississippi, two Mississippi...' he mentally counted.

There was obvious tension filling the room.

The old man, eyes alert, though edging toward opaque, looked up at the police officer. He cleared his throat, and studied the detective. "You have your warrant, Detective Sullivan," he whispered, "but be careful, young man; the press will eat us alive if you do not abide to the limited request."

Felix nodded again and slowly backed out of the master and commander's office without making a single sound.

After he closed the door, Felix took a deep breath and turned to the judge's assistant who smiled.

"You are a lucky man, Detective Sullivan," as she handed the officer the neatly printed warrant.

CHAPTER 12

The man was drawn to his favorite newsstand on the corner of Northwest second avenue and 67th street because it was ubiquitous and largely taken for granted. This Manhattan newsstands, a makeshift sidewalk store, sold candy, sodas, and lottery tickets, along with newspapers and magazines. Unfortunately, it was losing its vitality to the car culture, the allure of the internet, and the enticement of mobile phones resulting in the depressing epidemic of eyes glued to a screen syndrome.

"Thanks," the man said, with a bob of his shaggy head of hair and dark glasses, after purchasing the *Sunday Edition* of the New York Times. He immediately stopped mid-step and searched for the personal ads. He scanned down and smiled as he read; *24yo Iowa farm girl, who is also alone and lonely. Address to follow with correspondence.*

CHAPTER 13

Police Detective 2nd Grade Felix Muhammad Sullivan immediately went to the New York Times Newspaper where he proudly displayed the warrant. Several bigshots studied the document before having someone show him where the address and phone numbers were located for the personal ads' purchasers and responders to the listings. Sullivan was sweating like a stuck pig waiting for slaughter when he found what he was looking for.

The name that immediately pop up was a Gary Sawyer, or the name he used when placing the advertisement. According to the accounting department, he had placed the same ad for nearly four years, but after the initial ad, he paid cash and left no address. However, the man's address from four years ago was on North West

Cambridge Street.

Felix searched for any police records for a Gary Sawyer, but found nothing. However, when he checked who owned the house at 6755 North West Cambridge Street, it was listed under the name of Andrew Peck, age, 34.

Which was all the detective needed to place a surveillance team nearby to document who goes in and out. Therefore, a non-descript police vehicle and two plain-clothed police officers were ordered to keep an eye on the house until told otherwise.

CHAPTER 14

The surveillance team was stationed two blocks away from the house at 6755 North West Cambridge Street. The closest they could get without being observe by the suspect, who might be the *Sunday Edition* killer. All the team knew was someone in this area had placed an ad in the personals and that could be the killer.

"We're set here," the undercover policeman said into a microphone as the two kept their attention glued to the house. They would switch off using the binoculars for a clearer view.

After three days and nights, the one officer asked, "How long do we have to sit here?"

"Who knows?"

Static could be heard coming from the police

officer's microphone followed by a voice asking, "Anything?"

"Nah, not for the last couple of days. An old man with a walker comes out to get the paper or to hobbled to a nearby store for something, but other than that, nothing."

"Okay, wrap it up. I guess it was another false alarm again. Come on back to the station."

"Roger that, over and out."

29-year-old Gary Sawyer was the name and age he used when searching for his next victim and placing the newspaper ads in the Times and writing the letters to the women. He smiled as he peeked out of his modest home on North West Cambridge Street and watched the undercover policemen in the nondescript car drive off.

Andrew Peck was his real name, which was printed on his driver's license, and he would turn 34 years old on June 17th. "What's five fuckin' years. The younger girls don't like to date men over 30, so I help them along with their fantasies." He giggled at his cleverness as he watched out the window to make sure they had gone.

He absent-mindedly rubbed his chest, which still itched from the gynecomastia surgery five months ago.

The procedure was known as male breast reduction for

over-developed or enlarged breasts in men. He should have had it done when he was a teenager, but his parents wouldn't allow him to have procedure. They said his female breast would go away, but they didn't. As a result, every time he showered in high school, the other guys made fun of him, trying to fondle or pinch his chest. He hated his teenage years.

His attention turned back to the policemen in the car watching his house. 'Better not put in any ads in the Times for a couple of weeks,' he decided.

"I wonder how they decided to watch my house?" he pondered out loud, scrunching his face up like walnut. He moved the fake walker he used anytime he left the house no matter when. Next, he carefully put on an elderly man's wig and hat, bent glasses with black plastic frame, extra-large nondescript clothing purchased at a thrift store. And oversized shoes with a rock in the left one. 'I don't want to forget my limp while walking, so they do hurt my feet.' Cleaver!" he said to himself.

"Now, I look like all the other senior citizens making their way around the city. People who got close to him usually stepped back, for he smelled bad. 'Most old people smell bad,' he thought, and that was why he never washed his old codger clothes... so he would fit in better when he wore them out and about.

However, in his right-hand jacket pocket, was a Sig P365 9mm handgun and a rope, "Just in case," he whispered to himself grinning.

CHAPTER 15

Detective Sullivan noted the date of the personals, while skimming the long columns until he found what he was looking for.

The detective now knew the next young woman who answered the killer's ad was in eminent danger, and he was right.

Felix was immediately on his phone as he raced down the stairs leaving the rag. "Central, please send back up to 511 W 159th St, New York, NY. I believe a murder is about to take place!"

"Roger, back up on the way!"

Sullivan hit the sirens and red lights as he started the Ford Police Interceptor. Felix put the pedal to the metal spewing dirt, gravel and dust from the powerful 400-hp twin-turbo patrol vehicle tires screeching. The hopped-up police car squirmed like a trapped rattlesnake.

CHAPTER 16

It was the narrow moment between dusk and darkness, when the mailman finally delivered a letter to Hazel Hampton from the farming community of Le Claire, Iowa.

Her small apartment was on the second floor, with three wide windows overlooking the sidewalk and street below. She enjoyed watching the numerous pedestrians going about their busy lives. She wondered what their thoughts were as they rushed by going to wherever their legs would take them. Each New Yorker was in their own private world silenced by noise cancelling headphones or earbuds, while staring obsessively at their phone's screen clutched in their sweaty palms. They thought, they were the center of the universe, while ridiculously hopeful of getting another "like" on Facebook even though it was from a complete stranger they would never meet.

Hazel rushed down to check her mailbox. She peeked in, and sure enough, there was a letter... the fifth from a nice man named Gary Sawyer, or so he said. He also asked if she would keep his numbered letters together so she did. 'Strange?' she pondered, 'but what the heck, it's the city.'

She hurried out and down, and left the door open to her apartment, but being from Iowa; she did so out of habit; however, her next-door neighbor told her it was a bad idea.

The man made his way quietly into the room and to a closet after the woman went downstairs. He smiled a wicked smile of evil. 'This will be my 11th, or is it my 12th?' The killer nervously twisted the small rope in his hands. But he was always apprehensive before the kill.

CHAPTER 17

Hazel Hampton, from the quaint farming community of Le Claire, Iowa, stood in the middle of her tiny front room, took out a pocket knife she always carried, and slit open the letter excitedly, and started to read.

She glanced up and saw a reflection in the window of someone about to put his arm over her head and neck. Her automatic response was to raise her left hand as her father had always instructed when her brothers were about to choke her again.

Hazel left hand was up, surprising her attacker, for this had never happened before. Also, this woman was the same size he was or even a little bigger and was strong too, he soon found out.

The killer's rope was partway around her neck when she stabbed the man five times in his thigh with the pocket knife she was holding in her hand after opening the envelope. This ignited a horrific screech of pain and agony, causing the rope to slacken quickly.

Blood flowed profusely down the man's leg, causing him to loosen his grip, but he still clung to her back.

Hazel reached up and easily cut the rope, but the man still held tight to her shoulders. He actually pulled himself up and was now on her back as if she was giving him a piggyback ride.

Hazel could hear sirens in the distance as she glanced up and raced for the front window with all of her strength. She crashed through the glass and knew what was about to happen.

She turned mid-air and ended up landing squarely on her attacker's chest in the middle of the busy sidewalk with the killer underneath her. She landed directly on top of him, knocking the breath out of him thus he was unable to talk or breathe. Now there was blood all over the sidewalk from the stab wounds in his leg.

Hazel got up as several bystanders continued to gawk and take videos of what happened. She took her knife, slit the crotch of his trousers, pulled out his manhood, and cut off his testicles and penis at the same time, initiating another horrific scream from her attacker. She had helped her father castrate young bulls many times back in Iowa, the only difference here was she cut off everything.

The crowd was horrified as they watched the woman calmly slicing away. She stood up, his manhood in her hand, and walked over and tossed them into the sewer drainage in the street. Next, she went back, leaned down, and cut off the tip of his nose.

"Now, you son of a bitch, your ugly too, but maybe you can turn into a transgender person or something." She laughed at her morbid joke as she sat on the curb with the numerous people watching and recording. Hazel Hampton smiled back as they recorded her.

"One guy stepped forward and made a sarcastic remark, but he quickly backed off when she pointed at him with her knife and gruffed, "careful, ass hole, or you'll be next!"

The crowd laughed, Hazel grinned, but the man hurried away and didn't look back.

The woman from Iowa turned to the killer and

thought for a moment. "You better put pressure on what's left of your crotch otherwise you'll bleed out. Your choice."

The man was moaning and groaning but did what she suggested. You shouldn't have cut off everything!" he complained between whimpers and sobs.

"You shouldn't have tried to choke me to death with that garrote." She glanced over picked up the rope and placed it in her lap and waited for the authorities to arrive.

Moments later, several police vehicles arrived at the scene. The officers hurried out of their patrol cars and rushed over to the downed man and woman sitting on the curb smiling.

Police Detective 2nd Grade Felix Muhammad Sullivan was first to enter the area and kneeled and asked, "Are you Hazel Hampton from Iowa?"

"Yes, Sir," she answered politely, in a nervous voice nodding, but did not get up.

They both stood. Hazel Hampton's hands were trembling as she tucked in her shirt and brushed the glass off her trousers.

Police Detective 2nd Grade Felix Muhammad Sullivan signaled a patrolman with a motion to his mouth. A few minutes later, the officer came over and offered her a cup a of hot coffee, which she readily accepted.

"You were lucky," said Felix, watching the young woman regain her composure.

"The bastard tried to choke me to death with a rope, but I taught him a lesson he'll never forget!" She grinned.

"You were lucky. The other 11 were not."

"11?"

"11, and you would have been his 12th!"

"I guess I was lucky," she answered, "but he wasn't," replied the young lady. "This will teach him not to fuck with a 6-foot redhead from Iowa."

Felix smiled and glanced down at the man squirming and whimpering on the cement while holding his groin.

"I dare say he won't again."

THE AMBULANCE RIDE

The screaming sirens echoed between the buildings as the orange and white ambulance sped toward the hospital. Within the protective sanctuary of the rescue wagon were two paramedics working feverously to save a man's life.

"Call the ER and tell them we're losing him!"

The other man picked up the two-way and said, "ER central, A1 here, come in."

"Go ahead, A1."

"Need advice for a patient going bad," stated the paramedic into the microphone.

"One moment. Doctor Vance, here. What do you need?"

"Doc, our patient, is bleeding out; we need to infuse him with some blood."

"What are his vital and description of the patient?"

"BP 70 of 40, pulse 158 weak and thready."

"Do you have any O neg onboard?"

"Roger... two units. Currently, we're running two liters of Lactated Ringers wide open."

"Start the two units of the O neg and lower his head down and try to get here as quickly as you can!"

"Roger that. Oh, and Doc? This guy will need a urologist when we get there."

"A urologist?"

"Yes, someone cut off... well, everything!"

"Roger."

"Roger, A1 out."

Moments later, the medical technician's nightmare was about to end. The emergency room doors burst open as the rescue wagon raced in. The two medics opened the two back doors to the ambulance, seized the stretcher, and flipped the release lever allowing the cart's four rubber rollers to go into motion. They brought the litter out, down, and back up again, locking the aluminum braces to full extension in perfect unison. They raced toward the emergency department, narrowly missing the ER crew racing to assist.

The emergency room was a mass of confusion, with people running, lights blinking, bells ringing.

"What the heck is going on?" asked one of the ambulance's paramedics to a nurse.

"Covid, Covid, Covid! We've lost 57 patients today, and there will be more tomorrow. Most of them were unvaccinated... some people are such idiots; I can't believe it. We are all running on empty with no end in sight." She lowered her head and started to cry as she marched back into the main thrust of the Covid-19 oncoming fiasco that was consuming the staff and patients alike.

A disheveled, frazzled man raced over and looked at the patient. "I'm Vance; thanks for hurrying. Is he dead?"

"Close."

"We have a surgeon coming. He'll have to take care of this guy here. There is no room in the operating rooms or anywhere else for that matter. This place is full, including the hallway. If you don't think he'll make it roll him over there against the wall; that way he'll be out of the way until someone takes him to the morgue. Thanks, guys."

The ambulance crew immediately started to wheel the dying man against the far wall out of the way.

"Hey, Hank!" a man yelled to the other physician.

Vance turned back to the medics, "he's the urologist."

They nodded their heads. "Good luck, Doc!"

The man gave a halfhearted wave over his shoulder as he hurried back into the dragon's mouth of death.

The surgeon glanced at the patient, "Looks like he's dead. Vance said he bled out? What happened?"

"He tried to kill some woman, and she got the best of him and cut... well, cut everything off."

"Jesus!" the surgeon said, moving between the patient and another with Covid, who was dying. He turned to a passing nurse. "Nurse, I need some sutures, bandages, antibiotics, and Lidocaine."

She stopped mid-step and hesitated, "ah, okay, but I can't stay. You know that... right?"

"Zoo?"

"You got it, Doc, a zoo."

"No problem. Thank you, Ma'am, and I hope you get home sometime today."

She nodded and was gone again, hurrying back toward the dragon's mouth of horror. Now it was breathing fire in the form of Covid-19 and Covid Omicron while concocting any other variant, it could to wipe out as many unvaccinated as the beast could.

A half-hour later, the surgeon had closed the deep wound, infused antibiotics, and packed the crotch the best he could. He also sutured closed the five stab punctures in the man's right thigh.

A moment later, he hurried to the ER physician and said, "I'm out of here, Dr. Vance. Good luck."

"Thanks for your help. Is he going to make it?"

"Nope! I'm surprised he hasn't died before this. I check his hemoglobin, and it 7.gm/dl, which makes him teetering on the brink. But who knows? But I did go ahead and sign the death certificate with the cause of death as exsanguination. I figured that might help you a tad. Oh, the other Covid guy beside him passed too."

"This Covid crap is too much. The hospital is full the hallways are full. I've been here for 37 hours, and counting. We have patients dying right and left, and there is nothing we can't do a thing about it."

"Unvaccinated?"

"98 percent of them and then they have the audacity to ask if it's too late to get vaccinated?"

Vance glanced around and saw the patients stacking up like cords of wood in the ER and hallways too, with others waiting in the ambulances unable to enter, for the place was too full.

An hour later, Andrew woke with a start, shook his head, and was confused. He looked at the two IVs flowing into both of his arms and glanced around, and realized where he was. "Emergency room somewhere. God damn place looks busy," he said to himself, scanning the enclosed area.

He pulled the curtain around himself and changed into a clean hospital uniform lying on a nearby cart. Next, he put on a mask surgical cap and read the death certificate with his name on it. He added, cremate as soon as possible and scribble the same doctor's signature.

Next, he put the paper on the dead man beside him and got up, looking around. He was unsteady on his feet initially but held onto the stretcher for a moment. Andrew got a plastic garbage bag from a nearby cart, along with several ampules of antibiotics, more bandages, and some pain pills along with three more bags of fluid.

He put them into a plastic container and started to walk out but was stopped before he got to the door.

A nurse, whose name tag listed her as *Ms. Booker, ER Chief Nurse,* barked, "take that patient to the morgue and hurry back," she pointed to the man who had just died from Covid.

"Yes, Ma'am," returned Andrew as he went back to the deceased patient, covered him with a sheet and wheeled the litter out, and followed the arrows on the signs leading him to the *morgue.*

The hospital's morgue was packed with the dead as he maneuvered the cart in and around the other deceased.

Andrew thought for a brief moment, 'maybe they'll have money or at least enough to get me home again.'

And then he went through all of the dead's pockets and found a total of $732. He looked all around to make sure no one was watching as he put the money into the plastic bag he was carrying.

He noticed several of the dead were hospital staff workers. He found a male member's name tag, removed it, and clipped it to his shirt.

"Now I look official," he said, smiling for he was now wearing a mask, surgical cap, gown, and gloves, as were most of the staff. He hurried back toward the ER but walked out of the hospital feeling a little dizzy and sore but still alive. He immediately hailed a taxi which took him home.

"Stop here, please!" he instructed the driver who nodded.

Andrew was a block from his modest home on North West Cambridge Street but wanted to ensure no more policemen were there. He stood behind a tree and watched for any undercover officers in nondescript cars. After he felt relatively safe, he moved near several bushes to wait and watch longer, just in case, there were no police officers anywhere.

Peck did not want to go in the front door in case someone saw him, so he slowly made his way to the rear of the house.

He waited again then carefully opened the door into the dark home. The entry to the basement's stairs was near the backdoor thus it was easy for him to make his way to the basement without turning on any lights that curious onlookers might see.

His parents had built the house many years ago, and at that particular time, they installed a large old-fashion coal burning boiler to heat the home. But now, this archaic furnace was a relic. However, after his folk died, he cleaned out the inside of the huge steel incinerator, and cut a large exit in the back of the casing that was against the wall. Next, he constructed a door into a storage area and built and furnished the 10 feet by 10 feet space as a safe room that could only be accessed via the unused boiler.

Andrew furnished the tiny room with water, a toilet, a small frig, a TV, and a computer, along with enough food to last several months. And now he needed the safe space for a prolong period or until he completely healed.

BECOMING ANNA

The house smelled stale and old as he climbed back up the staircase, hesitating to turn on any lights until he became Anna, which he was more or less.

He quickly got onto the computer and had a will drawn up bequeathing everything in his bank accounts and home to his sister, Anna, who was nonexistent until now or would be when he was finished with the transgender modification.

Thus, after more than five months in the safe room, he decided to venture out but did so only at night for the first time. He went to a hotel and stayed until the following morning. At which time he took a taxi to the house and brazenly walked around in female attire, hoping all of the nosey neighbors would see him/her as Andrew's sister,

Anna, and they did.

Andrew contacted several surgeons, and after finding one, he was surprised when the doctor demanded full payment upfront. The physician specialized in performing sex-change operations. Andrew followed his orders and began taking the required feminizing hormone therapy to induce physical changes in his body to become a female.

The next thing was to have sex reassignment surgery, also known as gender reassignment surgery.

"What have I got to lose?" he looked down and could not help but chuckle. "The bitch!"

Six months later, he was a her or a more complete Anna Peck, Andrew's Sister.

During his to her transition, Anna ordered all the necessary womanly things she might need, and the clothing items she thought she should have. It wasn't easy, for he may look like a woman, but he would always be Andrew.

"Now, I've got to find out how to act like a female," he said, glancing at his computer. Everything is on Google, and it was.

It read *What type of woman do you want to be?*

In clothing, he leaned more towards 'femme' styles, which was more wearing dresses and skirts rather than trousers. He found out that femininity was not solely about external things, i.e., clothes, cosmetics, or posture; it was about attitude.

In any case, these theories soon became academic when he started living as a female: the abuse from men, however caused him far more concern, for it came as street harassment. When Andrew/Anna pulled out the Sig P365 9mm handgun, they quickly backed off, usually with derogatory comments.

ANOTHER DAY AT THE OFFICE

Detective 2nd Grade Felix Muhammad Sullivan smiled as he read the report regarding the *Sunday Edition* killer.

"Well? Whatcha grinning ear to ear about Irish?" Asked his partner, Detective 2nd Grade, Dombrowski.

"It always feels good to close a case that's been hanging over you for... well over four-fuckin' years. The bastard died in Saint Anthony's Emergency Department and cremated a day later."

"Couldn't happen to a better guy," returned Dombrowski shaking his head.

"Ya got that right," said Irish.

"What the fuck's going on in here, Irish, Dombrowski?" bellowed a loud, blustery voice of the precinct's Lieutenant Washington, a big black man who had been a policeman for nearly 30 years and counting.

"Ain't you guys got nothin' better to do now that your killer is dust?" he let out a deep, gravely laugh. "Good job, Irish. Oh, by the way, the Commissioner promoted you to Detective 1st Grade, which means ya gotta do paperwork rather than beatin' the bush for bad guys." The man walked off laughing.

"Detective 1st Grade?" gasped Irish.

"Yeah, Irish, and that means paperwork, which we all know you like," giggled Dombrowski.

SUNDAY EDITION **KILLER RETURNS**

Anna placed her first ad in the *Sunday Edition* personals that read, *Alone and lonely, 29yo trans female. Leave address and correspondence will follow.*

The killer smiled and put the rope in her purse as well as her Sig P365 9mm handgun just in case.

A BAD DAY AT THE OFFICE

You're not gonna like this, Boss," said Detective 2nd Grade, Dombrowski to Detective 1st Grade, Felix Muhammad Sullivan.

"What?" asked Irish.

Dombrowski handed his partner a copy of the New York Times. It read: *The **Sunday Edition** killer has returned,* followed by the gruesome details listing the murder of a young homosexual male being strangled with a rope after responding to a personal ad in the New York Time's

SUNDAY EDITION

THE END

www.ingramcontent.com/pod-product-compliance
Lightning Source LLC
Chambersburg PA
CBHW071344130726
47996CB00002B/826